THE SPY IN THE BLEACHERS
created by
GERTRUDE CHANDLER WARNER

Illustrated by Robert Papp

ALBERT WHITMAN & Company
Chicago, Illinois

Library of Congress Cataloging-in-Publication Data
is available from the Library of Congress.

The Spy in the Bleachers
Created by Gertrude Chandler Warner;
Illustrated by Robert Papp.

ISBN: 978-0-8075-7606-9 (hardcover)
ISBN: 978-0-8075-7607-6 (paperback)

Cover art by Robert Papp.

For information about Albert Whitman & Company,
visit our web site at www.albertwhitman.com.

The Boxcar Children Mysteries

Contents

THE SPY IN THE BLEACHERS

CHAPTER I

Cogwheel Stadium

"Wow!" said Benny. "Two baseball fields! One is on the outside, and another one's on the inside." Benny was six years old. He was excited that Grandfather was taking them to a baseball stadium. Not just for a day, but for a whole week!

Jessie, who was twelve, smiled at her younger brother. "There's nobody using the outdoor ball field right now," she said. "What does that make you think?" All four Alden children were good at solving mysteries, but

Jessie was the one who always listed the facts and what they meant.

"It makes me think we can use it right now," said Benny eagerly.

"Or, it makes me think we aren't allowed to use it," said ten-year-old Violet. She was the shyest of the Aldens. As she spoke she slipped a baseball glove onto her left hand.

"Who's right?" kidded Henry. "Benny or Violet?" Henry was fourteen and very good at figuring out how things worked. Sometimes he even invented his own tools. This time he said, "Look at the sign."

Grandfather parked the car in the big parking lot surrounding Cogwheel Stadium. They would stay at an inn here in the town of Clayton. And they would go to a baseball game every day.

The four Alden children lived with their grandfather, James Alden. After their parents had died, the children had run away from home and lived in the woods in an old boxcar. They had never met their grandfather and thought he would be mean. But their grandfather found them and they learned he was a good person.

All five Aldens climbed out of the car and looked at the sign. *Play Ball!* the sign said. *Whenever You Want To.*

"Benny is right," said Violet happily. "We can use the ball field!"

"After you're done," said Grandfather, "go to the front gate of the stadium. Tell them that Jim Tanaka left tickets for you."

Grandfather walked toward the front gate of Cogwheel Stadium. Henry, Jessie, Violet, and Benny took bats and balls and gloves onto the field.

"Jessie can pitch," said Henry, "and I'll catch. Violet and Benny can take turns hitting."

Violet turned to Benny. "You can bat first, and I'll try to catch what you hit. Then we can switch places."

Benny stood at the plate and Jessie threw the ball. Benny took a wide swing with the bat. He missed the ball.

"Watch the ball as it leaves Jessie's hand,"

Henry told him. "Just keep your eye on the ball, then hit it."

Benny watched the ball. When it came to him, he swung his bat. The bat hit the ball and the ball bounced across the infield. Violet ran to pick it up near first base.

"Good one," said Henry.

After Jessie threw twenty pitches to Benny, it was Violet's turn to bat.

Benny stood near second base and watched. He saw Henry had his catcher's mitt pointed down. His other hand was down, too. Henry was moving his fingers up and down, almost like he was counting. Benny saw one finger down, then two fingers down, then three fingers down. Then back to one finger.

"Hey!" said Benny. "What's Henry doing with his fingers?"

Jessie turned around to answer. "I want to practice my pitching, so Henry is giving me signs on what to throw."

"Signs?" asked Benny. "What kind of signs?"

"Signs with his fingers. One finger down

is a sign that he wants me to throw a fastball. Two fingers down is a sign that he wants me to throw a change-up."

"What's a change-up?" asked Benny.

"It looks just like a fastball, but comes in slower."

Benny thought about this. "When I watched the ball come out of your hand, sometimes it came fast. But sometimes I swung before the ball even got to me. That pitch must have been a change-up!"

"That's right," said Jessie. "If you had known the pitch was going to be a change-up, you would have been ready for it. You would have hit the ball." Jessie turned back to throw to Violet.

By now the parking lot was half full. The Aldens gathered their balls, bats, and gloves and put them in the car.

They four of them walked to the front gate of Cogwheel Stadium. "Look at the long line of cars waiting to park," said Violet.

"That's part of the reason Grandfather is here," Jessie reminded her. "So many people are coming to Cogwheel Stadium that Grandfather is going to help with plans to make the stadium bigger. It needs more parking spaces. And more seats."

When they reached the turnstile, Henry spoke to the man taking tickets. "We're the Aldens. Our grandfather told us that Mr. Jim Tanaka left tickets for us."

"Welcome," said the man as he let them through the turnstiles. "*I'm* Jim Tanaka, and here are your four tickets." He reached into his shirt pocket and pulled out the tickets.

"Thank you," said Jessie. "Do all baseball team owners stand at the front gate?"

Jim Tanaka laughed. "Not usually," he said. "I'm here because the stadium is so crowded we don't have enough help."

"We'll help," said Henry. "We're very good at helping."

"Oh, I couldn't ask you to help," said Mr. Tanaka. "You're my guests, and you're here to enjoy the game."

"But we enjoy helping," said Jessie. "Especially if our help is needed."

"I really do need help," Mr. Tanaka said. "Thank you for asking. You can start—Oh, hello."

Benny turned to see who Mr. Tanaka was talking to. It was a man dressed in shorts and a flowered shirt. He wore a Cogs baseball cap and sunglasses. The cap brim was pulled down so low that it hid the man's face. In his hand was a pencil and small notebook.

Instead of saying hello, the man raised a finger to his lips and whispered, "Shhhh!"

"Oh," said Jim Tanaka. "Right." He let the man through the turnstiles.

"Who was that?" asked Benny.

"Oh, uh, nobody," answered Jim Tanaka. "Now let me show you what you'll be doing." He looked at the children again. "Henry and Violet, I'm going to put you here, at the front gate, just behind the ticket takers."
He walked over to a large cardboard box and reached in. He pulled out something large and orange. "These are today's giveaways," Mr. Tanaka explained. "I want you to give one to each person who comes in."

"This is great," said Henry. "It's a foam glove shaped like a cog!" Henry put a hand into a glove and waved it around.

"The fans love these free gloves," Mr. Tanaka said. "When the Cogs are winning, everybody wears a glove and waves it in the air."

Benny could see that the word *Cogs* was written on the orange shape. "What's a cog?" he asked.

"A cog is a gear," Mr. Tanaka answered. "It's a circle made out of metal. Old cogs used to be made out of wood."

Benny looked at the foam shape. "What are all those bumps sticking out around the cog?"

"Those are called teeth," Henry explained. "If you put two gears together, the teeth of one slide into the spaces of the other. That way, one gear turns the other gear."

"Like on our bikes!" said Benny excitedly.

"That's right," said Mr. Tanaka. "Many, many years ago the town of Clayton was a cog-making center. That's why my team is called the Clayton Cogwheels. 'Cogs' for short."

Mr. Tanaka spoke to Jessie and Benny. "We'll leave Henry and Violet here to hand out foam gloves. The two of you follow me, please. I'll take you to where you can help."

Henry and Violet watched Jessie, Benny, and Mr. Tanaka walk through the crowd. Then they began to give out free foam gloves as the fans came through the turnstile.

"Oh, thank you!" said one fan. "My son and daughter love the Cogs." Violet watched the mother, son, and daughter each put on a Cogs glove and wiggle it.

"This is fantastic!" another fan said to Henry. "The Cogs finished first last year. And it looks like they'll win the pennant again this year."

"That's for sure," said the next fan in line. "Only five games left to go, all of them here in Cogwheel Stadium."

Violet knew that was good news. When a team played on their home field, they had a better chance of winning.

"How many games do the Cogs have to win in order to win the pennant?" she asked Henry.

"Only two," Henry answered. "If the Cogs win two of these last five games, they win the pennant."

"The Cogs aren't going to win two of the last five games," called out a young man who had overheard them. He wore a Hatters baseball cap. "The Hatters will win all five and win the pennant. Go, Hatters!" he shouted as he walked by.

"Look at all the Hatters baseball caps coming our way," whispered Henry. "There are as many Hatters fans here as there are Cogs fans."

A young woman taking tickets at the turnstile smiled at Henry and Violet. "The Hatters are from Madison, which is the next town over. The Hatters and Cogs have been rivals for over a century."

"Wow!" breathed Henry. "These should be very exciting games!"

Violet watched a young woman come

through the turnstile. The woman had long
blonde hair that she wore in braids. She was
dressed in a white T-shirt, denim shorts,
and white sneakers. Was she a Cogs fan or
a Hatters fan? She wore a visor instead of a
cap. The visor didn't say anything. Around
her neck the young woman had a pair of
binoculars.

Violet held out a free glove.

The woman took the foam glove from
Violet and tore it in half. Then she threw
the two halves on the ground and stomped
on them. "I hate the Cogs!" she shouted.
"They're a rotten, no-good team! I hope that
Cody Howard hits four home runs! I hope
the Cogs lose every one of the five games!"
The woman stomped away, into the crowd.

"Whoa!" said Henry. "She's a Hatters fan,
for sure."

Violet picked up the two halves of the
foam glove and threw them into a trash
barrel. "Who's Cody Howard?" she asked
her brother.

"He plays center field for the Hatters,"

Henry answered. "He's a great hitter. He might win the league batting title this year." Henry explained to Violet that each year the batting title was won by the player who had the highest batting average.

"Does that mean the player who has the most hits in a season?" asked Violet.

"Yes," answered Henry.

"Whoever wins the batting title wins a brand new car," said a man with a Cogs baseball cap. "I hope it's not Cody Howard," he said.

"Because he's a Hatter?" Henry asked the fan.

"Yeah," answered the fan. "I'd like to see the Cogs catcher, Reese Dawkins, win the title and the car."

Henry and Violet handed out free foam gloves until there weren't any left.

CHAPTER 2

View from the Bleachers

While Henry and Violet were giving out free gloves, Jessie and Benny followed Mr. Tanaka. Thousands of fans crowded the open area inside the stadium. Jessie saw that the fans were buying pennants and T-shirts and caps. Benny saw that the fans were buying food: hot dogs and popcorn and ice cream.

They followed Mr. Tanaka through an unmarked door. Now they stood inside a very large kitchen. Men and women in white aprons were cooking hundreds of hot dogs on grills. Others were putting the dogs into buns and wrapping them in clean paper. Still others were filling large paper boxes full of popcorn.

"This is a very busy place," Jessie said. "Everybody is working hard."

"Yes," replied Mr. Tanaka. "Cogs fans are hungry fans."

Benny stood still, staring at all the food.

Jim Tanaka looked down at him. "I'll bet you're hungry," he said.

Benny looked up. "How did you know?" he asked.

"I have a grandson your age," said Mr. Tanaka. "He's always hungry." Mr. Tanaka grabbed two large boxes of popcorn off a counter. He handed one to Jessie and one to Benny. "Eat some popcorn," he said, "and follow me around this room. I'll explain how you can help."

"Thank you," said Jessie as she took her box of popcorn.

"Thank you," said Benny. He shoved a

large handful of popcorn into his mouth. "Yum," he said.

Mr. Tanaka pointed to a metal door, not the one they had come through. "See all the vendors coming through that door?" he asked. Then he looked down at Benny. "A vendor is somebody who sells things."

"Like popcorn," said Benny, eating another large handful.

"Yes," answered Mr. Tanaka. "Some vendors sell food. Others sell baseball caps or pennants."

"Souvenirs," said Jessie.

"That's right," said Mr. Tanaka. He looked at them. "Would you rather help with the food or the souvenirs?"

"The food!" answered Benny right away.

Jim Tanaka laughed. "I thought so. Follow me."

Jessie and Benny followed him to one side of the large kitchen. Workers were putting just-cooked hot dogs in paper wrappers.

"Jessie, do you think you can wrap these hot dogs and stack them inside these vendor boxes?" asked Mr. Tanaka.

"Yes," said Jessie. "I can do a good job at that." She began to wrap and stack hot dogs.

"Very good," Mr. Tanaka said. "I really appreciate your help."

"You're welcome," said Jessie. In no time at all, she had filled one vendor box. As soon as she closed the lid on the box somebody took it from her. It was a young man.

"Hello, Carlos," Mr. Tanaka said to him. "I'd like you to meet Jessie Alden and her brother Benny. They volunteered to help us out today. Jessie and Benny, this is Carlos Garcia."

Jessie and Benny said hello to Carlos.

Benny stared at Carlos' baseball cap. A tall stiff wire stood up at the back of his cap, like an antenna. At the top of the wire was a Cogs pennant.

"Nice to meet you," said Carlos as he hurried away with a full box of hot dogs.

"Carlos is one of our best vendors," Mr. Tanaka said. "He works the bleachers, right where you'll be sitting."

"We'll buy our hot dogs from Carlos, then," said Jessie.

"Carlos will be easy for you to find," said Mr. Tanaka. "He wears that tall wire and pennant just so hungry fans can spot him. I sit in the owner's box near home plate—even I can see Carlos in the bleachers."

Before he left, Mr. Tanaka showed Benny how to load trays with boxes of popcorn. Benny liked this job.

Jessie loaded more boxes with hot dogs. Soon Carlos Garcia was back.

"You sell your hot dogs really fast," Jessie said.

Carlos laughed. "I'm a very good vendor," said Carlos. "But I'm an even better catcher." He frowned. "Better than Reese Dawkins, that's for sure."

"Who's Reese Dawkins?" asked Jessie.

"He's the Cogs catcher," explained Carlos. "And he doesn't know which pitches to call." Carlos picked up a full box of hot dogs and left.

Jessie was happy that she was able to help

Mr. Tanaka. Helping other people felt good. Soon one of the cooks came up to Jessie and Benny. "Thank you," he said. "Now you can go enjoy the game."

Jessie and Benny hurried out the door. Once again they were in the middle of thousands of fans. The two of them walked slowly, moving between groups of people.

They almost walked into the back of a large, fuzzy, orange circle. It was taller than Jessie. It had two legs that stuck out of the bottom. It had two arms which stuck out of the sides. It was a person in a big, strange costume!

"What's that?" asked Benny. "It has those things sticking out of it. Teeth, that's what they're called."

"Yes," said Jessie. "It looks like a giant walking cog. I'll bet it's the team mascot." Jessie had seen other sports mascots. They were people who wore big, fuzzy costumes.

Suddenly a group of children older than Benny ran up to the giant walking cog. "Wheelie!" they shouted, "Wheelie!" The cog turned around and around, bowing to the children.

Jessie saw words written across the front of the costume: *Wheelie the Cogwheel.*

As Benny and Jessie watched, Wheelie did a little dance for the children. Then he bowed to them again and continued walking.

"Let's stay behind Wheelie," said Benny. "I like to watch him."

Benny watched the fans. They held things out to Wheelie—napkins, pieces of paper, baseballs, and caps. One of them gave Wheelie a pen and the mascot autographed a napkin. After he autographed the napkin, the mascot held out a hand. The fan walked away.

Next Wheelie autographed a baseball. Once again he held out his hand. Benny saw the man with the autographed baseball put money into Wheelie's hand. Quickly, Wheelie's hand disappeared into his costume. Then it came out again, empty.

Just as Benny was about to tell Jessie what he saw, he heard cheering. Wheelie was racing down the aisle toward the playing field. Everyone was clapping and cheering to watch Wheelie run.

"Look," said Jessie, staring at the aisle number. "This is our section."

Jessie and Benny walked down the aisle, looking at row numbers. "I think we're way at the bottom," said Jessie. "We'll be very close to the baseball field." She was excited.

"I see Henry and Violet!" shouted Benny. He pointed to the second row of seats, where Henry and Violet sat.

"We just got here," Violet told Jessie and Benny. "We handed out all the foam gloves."

"I filled trays with popcorn boxes," Benny answered. "I could hardly keep up!"

"And I wrapped hot dogs and put them into vendor boxes," answered Jessie.

"I'm hungry," said Benny, looking around.

"Me, too," said Henry. "It's way past lunch time."

Jessie looked around, then smiled. She had spotted a pennant that seemed to float in the air. But she could tell that it was attached to a wire, and the wire was attached to a baseball cap. "Carlos!" she shouted.

"Who are you calling?" asked Henry.

"Carlos Garcia," said Jessie. "He's a hot dog vendor."

In no time at all Carlos reached their seats. The children bought hot dogs. Henry paid for the hot dogs and also gave Carlos a tip.

"Thanks," said Carlos. He added the money to a large stack of bills in his hand.

Henry noticed that the top of the stack had one-dollar bills. He thought he saw a hundred-dollar bill on the bottom. *If that's a hundred*, thought Henry, *somebody bought a lot of hot dogs!*

The children ate their hot dogs and looked all around.

Henry looked at the baseball field and the players. He could see home plate clearly. He would have a great view of each pitch as it crossed the plate.

Jessie looked for Wheelie. At last she spotted him. The mascot was so close! The first row, right in front of them, was filled

with fans. Wheelie was sitting just past the fans. His chair was on a long platform built just below the front row of seats. Jessie thought that the mascot had the best view in all of Cogwheel Stadium.

Violet was looking around at all the people. Many of them wore Cogs baseball caps. But almost as many wore Hatters baseball caps. Violet looked at her own baseball glove, which she had brought into the stadium. She would love to catch a home run ball. After Violet finished eating her hot dog, she slipped off her free Cogs glove and put it beside her. She put on her real baseball glove. Shyly, she kept her gloved hand on her lap, where nobody could see it.

Benny wanted to look everywhere! He wanted to see the baseball players. He wanted to see Wheelie. He wanted to see and hear all the people. And he wanted to keep Carlos and the hot dogs in sight.

"Can you see?" Henry asked his brother.

"I can see everything," said Benny. "At first I thought these seats were too far away, but now I like them."

The person in front of Benny turned around and smiled at him. "Bleacher seats are the best seats in the whole park," she told him. "From the bleachers you have the best view of the whole game. Especially home plate." She looked at Violet. "And in the bleachers you might be able to catch a home run ball!"

Violet looked at Henry, and Henry looked at Violet. They both recognized the young woman. She was the one who had torn the free glove in half and then stomped on it. Henry was surprised that she seemed such a happy, friendly person. He was even more surprised that she was wearing a Cogs baseball cap!

"I'm Henry Alden," he told her. "These are my sisters, Violet and Jessie, and my brother Benny. We're from Greenfield. This is our first time at Cogwheel Stadium."

"I'm Emma Larke," the young woman said. "Clayton is my home town."

"Are you a Cogs fan?" asked Violet, staring at Emma's baseball cap.

"I was," she answered. "I was a Cogs fan from the time I was five years old. But now I hate the Cogs," she said with a frown. "Especially Reese Dawkins, who's a horrible catcher."

Benny was confused. "But you're wearing a Cogs baseball cap," he said to Emma.

"Oh," she said, touching the brim of her cap. "I forgot." She took the cap off and put it in her canvas bag. Then she put a visor on and turned to face the field.

"Carlos Garcia doesn't like Reese Dawkins, either," Jessie told Henry and Violet. "He said so when I was loading hot dogs into his vendor box."

The Hatters batted first. Emma Larke jumped up and cheered every Hatter. The Cogs' pitcher struck out two of them. The third one grounded out to first.

Each time a Hatter made an out, Wheelie stood up and pumped his fists.

"The Cogs look like a good team," Jessie said.

The Cogs weren't able to score in the first

inning. Emma stood up and cheered each time a Cogs batter made an out.

"Hey, you!" yelled a fan several rows back. "Sit down!"

Between innings, Wheelie stood up and entertained the fans. First he puffed out his chest and strode back and forth on the platform. Then he pointed to the Hatters dugout and pinched his nose together with two fingers. Cogs fans cheered because Wheelie was telling them that the Hatters stank.

In the top of the second inning Cody Howard came to bat for the Hatters. Henry noticed that Cody batted left-handed, and the Cogs pitcher threw right-handed. Left-handed batters usually did well against right-handed pitchers.

Wheelie held his nose.

Emma stood up. She took off her visor and waved it in the air. "Go, Cody!" she shouted.

The pitch came in and Cody Howard blasted the ball into the bleachers. The home run sailed over their heads.

"Wow," said Jessie, "he guessed right on that pitch."

"Yes," said Henry. "It was a fastball."

The score was now 0-1. The Hatters were winning.

The next two Hatter players struck out swinging. Each time, Wheelie stood up and pretended to faint, as if their swings knocked him down.

Benny was having a great time. He loved seeing everything that was happening. He saw Carlos come down the aisle with two hot dogs in his hand. Carlos leaned over the rail and gave the two hot dogs to Wheelie.

Violet was also watching Carlos Garcia. She loved the way his orange Cogs pennant swayed on its wire. She saw Carlos take an envelope out of his pocket and give it to Wheelie. Carlos was frowning as he walked back up the aisle.

Jessie watched the game closely. From where she was sitting, she had a perfect view of the catcher. She could see Reese Dawkins put down one finger, then two, then three.

Although the Cogs got runners on base, they didn't score. At the top of the fifth inning, Cody Howard came to bat again.

Emma Larke stood up. She took her visor off, then put it on backwards. "Go, Cody!" she shouted again.

Wheelie stood up and stretched. He held his hand to his mouth like he was yawning. He sat back down.

Carlos stood at the railing behind Wheelie. He opened his metal vendor's box. He slammed its lid up and down three times.

The Cogs pitcher threw the ball and Cody Howard hit it the length of the park! Violet saw the ball coming their way. Everybody stood up to catch it. Violet saw the ball getting closer and closer—she reached for it with her baseball glove.

Violet felt the baseball land in her glove. *I caught it!* she thought. *I caught it!*

"Great catch!" shouted Henry.

"Wow!" said Jessie, patting her sister on the back. "That was terrific."

All the fans cheered.

Violet smiled shyly. She looked at the beautiful white baseball she had caught, turning it around in her hands.

"Can I see it?" asked Benny.

"Sure," said Violet, handing the ball to Benny.

Emma Larke turned around. "That was a very nice catch!"

"Thank you!" said Violet.

"You were smart to bring your glove," Carlos told her. "A good ballplayer is always ready."

Then Carlos frowned. "That's a second home run for Cody. He hit it because Reese Dawkins called the wrong pitch."

"The pitcher threw a curveball," said Henry, who had been watching closely.

"That's right," said Carlos. "And Cody hit it out of the ballpark. The Hatters are now leading, two-nothing."

"What do you think the pitcher should have called?" asked Jessie.

"A change-up," said Carlos. "Reese Dawkins called the wrong pitch." He banged the lid to his hot dog box a couple of times and walked away.

Everybody sat down again.

"That was a great catch, Violet," said Henry. "What a great souvenir of Cogwheel Stadium."

Violet grinned. "I'm going to put the baseball on my bookshelf at home."

Henry looked at Jessie. "Cody Howard acted like he knew what pitch was coming."

Jessie nodded. She remembered what she'd told Benny about the way catchers made signals to pitchers. The batter of the other team wasn't supposed to know what those signals were—but did Cody Howard know?

"I hope this isn't what it looks like," Jessie said to Henry.

The Cogs players tried to score, but didn't. In the top of the eighth inning, Cody Howard came to bat again.

Emma Larke turned around. "Cody is going to win the batting championship," she told the Aldens. "And Reese Dawkins *isn't!*" She clapped her hands.

Cody stepped up to the plate, the Cogs pitcher threw the ball, and Cody Howard hit it out of Cogwheel Stadium.

"It is what it looks like," Henry said to Jessie quietly.

Jessie nodded. "Somebody is stealing the signs Reese Dawkins is giving the pitcher."

"And that somebody is signaling the signs to Cody Howard," said Henry.

At the end of nine innings, the Cogs lost, 0-3. Cody Howard scored all three of the Hatters' runs.

"This is bad," said Henry. "Unless the sign-stealing stops, the Cogs might lose all five games. That means they would lose the pennant."

CHAPTER 3

Next to the Dugout

The next morning Grandfather drove the children to Cogwheel Stadium. He parked in the same spot as before. "I'll bet you want to play more ball today," he said.

"Actually, we want to help Mr. Tanaka as much as we can," said Jessie. Last night after dinner she and Henry had told Benny and Violet about the sign stealing. Now all four children wanted to find out who was stealing Reese Dawkins's signs and signaling them to Cody Howard.

Grandfather led them to the owner's office on the upper level of Cogwheel Stadium.

"Good morning," said Jim Tanaka. "Did you enjoy yesterday's game, even though we lost?" he asked.

"Yes," said Benny. "I love the bleachers."

"We had a very good time," said Jessie. "Thank you so much for the tickets. And we would like to help you today, if you still need help."

"I would love more help," replied Mr. Tanaka. "Henry and Benny, Wheelie could use your help. And Jessie and Violet, I've got a job for you too."

* * * *

Wheelie the mascot had his own small dressing room. The man who played the mascot was dressed in cargo shorts, a T-shirt, and socks. "I'm Winn Winchell," he told Henry and Benny. "Call me Winn when I'm not in costume. When I'm in costume, call me Wheelie."

"You talk!" said Benny.

"Yep," said Winn. "I talk when I'm Winn.

I don't talk when I'm Wheelie."

"Why?" asked Benny.

"Because cogwheels don't talk, that's why," answered Winn. He took the bottom half of the orange Wheelie costume off its hook.

Henry watched Winn step into the bottom half of the costume. Henry saw suspenders hanging from it. He grabbed the suspenders and held them up for Winn.

"You're a quick learner," said Winn. He pulled the suspenders over his shoulders. "See that box in the corner?"

Henry and Benny looked where Winn was pointing.

"Those are rolled-up T-shirts," Winn told them. He handed Henry a large canvas bag. "Stuff as many of them in here as you can," he said. "When I go out on the field, you carry the bag and follow me. You hand me one T-shirt at a time, and I throw it to a fan. Got that?"

"Yes," said Henry. *This is cool*, he thought. *I get to walk on the baseball field!*

Winn handed Benny a canvas bag, too.

"Plastic water bottles," he said. "You carry this bag and follow behind Henry. Sometimes I give away shirts, and sometimes I give away bottles."

"Now listen carefully," he told them. "Whenever we're out of T-shirts or water bottles, you let me know. That's when we come back here and take a break. And as soon as we get back here, you help me take off the top half of my costume. And then you hand me a tall glass of ice water. Immediately." Winn pointed to a small refrigerator in the corner." He looked at Henry and Benny. "Any questions?"

Henry and Benny shook their heads.

"Good," said Winn, "because Wheelie doesn't talk." He took the top half of his Wheelie costume from its hook and began to slip it over his head.

Henry helped Winn, who became Wheelie. Wheelie turned in a circle, then faced the door. He made a come-with-me motion with his arm. Henry and Benny grabbed their canvas bags. They followed Wheelie onto the baseball field.

As soon as he walked onto the baseball field, Wheelie turned three cartwheels. The fans cheered.

Henry was surprised at how loud the crowd noise was. Really loud! *So this is what baseball players hear*, he thought.

Wheelie waved his arms to the fans and they shouted louder. Henry followed the mascot as he walked around the field, close to the stands. Each time Wheelie threw a free T-shirt into the crowd, Henry handed him another one. And when he threw a plastic water bottle, Benny ran up with his canvas bag of bottles.

When they were out of T-shirts they went back to the dressing room. Henry helped take off the top half of Wheelie's costume. Benny poured a glass of ice water and handed it to the mascot.

Winn drank the entire glass of water. He handed the empty glass to Benny. "It's hot inside this costume," he said. He reached into the bottom half of the costume and pulled out a bandana. An envelope fell out of the bandana onto the floor. Money fell out of the envelope and scattered everywhere.

Benny stooped to pick up the money. He saw one-hundred dollar bills!

"Don't touch that!" shouted Winn. He bent down and pushed Benny aside.

Benny didn't like being pushed. He thought Winn was rude.

Henry bent down behind Winn and picked up the envelope. The word Wheelie was handwritten on it, in big letters. The handwriting slanted toward the left.

"Is that the money you charge for an autograph?" Benny asked.

"Mind your own business," said Winn as he grabbed the envelope out of Henry's hand. Winn stuffed the money back into the envelope. Then he pushed the envelope down into his pockets.

Henry stood up and pulled a sheet of paper out of his pocket and held it out toward the mascot. "Could I have your autograph?" Henry asked.

Winn looked at the piece of paper. "Ill give you an autograph if you give me ten dollars."

"Oh," said Henry, taking back his paper. "Let me think about it."

Henry now knew that the mascot wanted ten dollars for an autograph. But the envelope had been full of one-hundred-dollar bills. The money in the envelope wasn't for autographs. *What is it for, then?* thought Henry. *And why did Winn get so upset about it?*

"Fill up your canvas bags," Winn told Henry and Benny. "We go out the door again in five minutes."

* * * *

Jessie and Violet were helping out in the large open area behind the bleachers. A small waterfall had been built there. Fans could walk into it and cool off on really hot days. Jessie and Violet helped the line of people move along. Violet kept the line straight and alongside the wall. Jessie let everybody have one minute under the waterfall, then it was the next person's turn.

"Time's up," said Jessie to a girl who was

about Benny's age.

"*Awww*," said the girl as she stepped out of the waterfall.

"You can get back in line and do it again," said Jessie with a smile. She watched as the girl ran to the back of the long line and stood there, dripping wet. There were other dripping wet people in line, too.

"It's so hot," said Violet. "I feel like walking through the waterfall myself, just to cool off."

"The waterfall is a wonderful idea," said Jessie. "Mr. Tanaka makes sure the fans have a lot of fun."

Violet nodded, then frowned. "I hope the Cogs win today. Maybe the sign stealer won't be here today."

Violet noticed a woman wearing a lavender dress. Violet loved all shades of purple and always noticed them. But she wondered why somebody would wear such a beautiful, dressy dress to a ballgame.

The woman had long blonde hair that curled up at the ends. She wore a straw hat with a wide brim.

The woman turned around. It was Emma Larke.

Emma didn't notice Violet or Jessie or even the waterfall. She seemed to be looking around for something, or somebody.

"Look," Violet said to her sister. "It's Emma Larke. She looks so different from yesterday. Let's say hello."

But just then Carlos Garcia walked up to Emma. He didn't notice Jessie or Violet, either.

"Reese Dawkins looked bad yesterday," the sisters heard Carlos say to Emma.

"Yes, but he's still playing today," answered Emma.

"The manager doesn't want to switch catchers this late in the season," said Carlos. "But next year—next year will be different."

Emma opened her straw handbag and pulled out her binoculars. She showed them to Carlos.

As Emma was showing the binoculars to Carlos, Violet saw Carlos pull an envelope from his pocket. Violet noticed handwriting on the envelope, but she couldn't see what it said. She saw Carlos drop the envelope into Emma's purse.

Carlos turned and saw her. "Hello, Violet," he said. "What are you doing?"

"Hello," said Violet. "We're helping out with the waterfall shower."

Emma turned, too, and said hello to Violet and Jessie. "I would have gone into the waterfall yesterday," she said, "but I don't want to get my clothes wet today."

"That's a beautiful dress," said Violet.

Emma twirled around, to show off her dress. "Thank you," she said. Emma reached into her straw purse and pulled out a pair of white lace gloves. She put them on and wiggled her fingers. Then Emma and Carlos walked away from the waterfall.

Violet saw them talking as they left. She wondered about Emma's binoculars. She wondered even more about Emma's white lace gloves.

* * * *

All four children met up in the aisle and walked down to their seats.

"Mr. Tanaka has given us tickets in the very first row," Jessie said.

"Right next to the Cogs dugout," Henry pointed out.

Benny stopped just before they entered their row. "Look," he said.

Jessie, Violet, and Henry looked. There was one other person in their row. He was sitting right next to the Cogs dugout. He wore dark sunglasses and a Cogs baseball cap pulled low. He wore shorts and a flowered shirt, and he was writing something in a small notebook. It was the man who had entered the turnstile yesterday. He had whispered "*Shhh*" to Mr. Tanaka.

Henry led the way into the row and sat beside the man with the notebook. "Hello," said Henry. "I'm Henry Alden, and these are my sisters, Jessie and Violet, and my brother Benny."

"Pleased to meet you," said the man as he put away his notebook. "You look like a happy group. How did you get these great seats?"

"Mr. Tanaka gave them to us," answered Jessie.

The man nodded. "That's just like Jim Tanaka. Very generous. Are you friends of his?"

"Our grandfather is helping Mr. Tanaka expand the seating and parking for Cogwheel Stadium," said Henry.

"And we're helping Mr. Tanaka, too," said Benny. "Today Henry and I helped Wheelie."

"Aha!" said the man. "I thought the two of you looked familiar. You were on the field handing Wheelie T-shirts and water bottles." He pulled his notebook out of his shirt pocket. He wrote something in it quickly, then put it back into his pocket.

Jessie had been waiting for the man to introduce himself, but so far he hadn't. "What should we call you?" she asked him.

The man turned to look at them. That was when Henry noticed the small headphone the man was wearing. His base-ball cap hid most of the headphone, but a small part could be seen.

"Do any of you like mysteries?" the man asked.

The children nodded. "We all like mysteries," Violet told him.

"Excellent," he replied. "Then you can call me 'Mr. X.' And now," he said, "the game is about to begin."

All four of the Aldens looked at Mr. X as he wrote something in his small notebook. Then he spoke softly into his headphone. Not even Henry, who was sitting right next to him, heard what he said.

The Cogs scored two runs in the bottom of the first inning. That made the Aldens very happy. That seemed to make Mr. X happy, too. He cheered the Cogs loudly.

Benny was starting to feel hungry. He wished Carlos Garcia were here to sell them hotdogs. Benny looked across the baseball field, into the bleachers. It didn't take him long to spot the tall pennant that Carlos wore on his head. "I can see Carlos!" he told Violet.

Violet looked in the direction Benny was

pointing. She saw Carlos give something to Wheelie. Probably a hot dog or a soft drink. She saw Emma Larke sitting in the front row of the bleachers. Emma's straw hat and lavender dress and white gloves made her very easy to see.

The second inning started. Cody Howard was the first man up for the Hatters. Henry tried to watch everything at once. He saw Wheelie hold his nose. He saw Emma Larke stand up and take off her straw hat. She waved it back and forth. Henry couldn't hear her from across the ballpark but he thought she must be shouting, "Go, Cody!"

Jessie was watching Carlos Garcia. When Cody came to bat, Carlos did not sell hot dogs. Carlos stood near the railing and watched Cody bat. She saw Carlos lift the lid of his vendor's box up and down.

The pitch came in and Cody Howard swung. Everybody heard a loud crack as the ball sailed out of Cogwheel Stadium.

"That proves it!" shouted a loud, angry voice. "Somebody is telling that batter what our pitching signals are! I want to know who is doing it!" Henry leaned over to see partway into the Cogs dugout. The person doing the shouting was Sam Jackson, the Cogs manager.

Mr. X spoke into his headphones and wrote something in his notebook.

"This is bad," Henry whispered to his sisters and brother. "We have to discover who is giving Cody Howard the Cogs' signals."

Jessie, Violet, and Benny nodded. Whoever was stealing signs was not a good sport.

The score remained Cogs 2, Hatters 1, until the top of the fifth inning, when Cody Howard hit another home run. The Hatters had a runner on, so now the Hatters were leading 3-2.

After Cody's second home run, Mr. X wrote for a long time in his notebook. Henry saw that Mr. X was right-handed.

Mr. X looked up from his notebook. "You kids say that you like mysteries," he said. "Well, here's a good mystery for you—there's a spy in the bleachers."

"A spy who is stealing Reese Dawkins' signs to the pitcher," said Jessie.

Mr. X looked surprised. "Say," he said, "you kids really are into mysteries, aren't you?"

The Aldens nodded.

"Well," said Mr. X, "I know who the spy is."

"You do?" asked Violet.

Mr. X nodded, then pointed across the baseball field into the bleachers. "It's the woman in the lavender dress," he said.

"How do you know she's the spy?" asked Violet.

"Obvious," said Mr. X. "She has binoculars so she can see the catcher's signs better. Then, each time Cody Howard is at bat, she stands up. She waves her visor or her straw hat or whatever she's wearing. That's how she signals Cody. Today she's wearing white lace gloves. Very suspicious, don't you think? So easy for the batter to see her hands."

In the bottom of the sixth inning, the Cogs scored two more runs to tie the score, 4-4.

But in the top of the seventh inning, Cody Howard came to bat again. Emma Larke stood up again and waved her straw hat. Cody did not hit a home run this time. But he did hit a triple, which allowed one of the Hatters already on base to score a run. The Hatters won the game, 5-4.

CHAPTER 4

In the Owner's Office

When the game was over, the children walked back to Mr. Tanaka's office.

Grandfather was there with Jim Tanaka, who looked very unhappy.

"Mr. Tanaka," said Henry. "The Cogs lost the last two games because somebody is stealing the catcher's signs."

"And that somebody is signaling the signs to Cody Howard," added Jessie. "That's why he hit five home runs and a triple in just two games. Because he knows. "

Mr. Tanaka rubbed his chin. "Well," he said slowly, "Cody Howard is a *very* good hitter. And he wants to win the batting title. Maybe that's why he hit all these home runs."

"It's true that Cody is a very good hitter," said Henry. "But he hit each of those home runs as if he knew *exactly* what pitch was coming."

Mr. Tanaka turned to Grandfather. "Your grandchildren are very, uh, unusual," he said.

"My grandchildren are very smart," said Grandfather. "They think things through. If they say somebody is stealing signs, they are most likely right."

"Hmmmm," said Mr. Tanaka, rubbing his chin again. "This is a very serious charge. Stealing signs is a very dirty trick."

Violet nodded. "It's not fair," she said.

"Hmmmm," Mr. Tanaka muttered again. He was about to reply, when the door opened with a bang.

Sam Jackson, the Cogs manager, burst into the office. "Somebody is stealing our signs!" he shouted. "That's why we lost these two games."

Before Mr. Tanaka could say anything, Wheelie came in just behind Sam. He was struggling to take off the top half of his costume. Sam Jackson turned around and helped him. "I told you this is none of your business," the manager said to the mascot.

"It *is* my business," replied Winn. "If somebody is stealing signs, I want to know who it is."

"*Your* job is to turn cartwheels," said Sam Jackson. "You stay out of this."

Mr. Tanaka raised a hand. "Quiet!" he said firmly.

The manager and the mascot stopped arguing.

"Sam," said Mr. Tanaka, "please continue with what you were saying."

"I tell you, somebody is stealing our signs! If we don't find out who it is and stop them, we're not going to win *any* of these five games. And you know we need to win *two games* to win the pennant." The manager looked at the Aldens. "What are these kids doing here?"

Mr. Tanaka introduced the children and Grandfather to Sam Jackson. "Henry, Jessie, Violet, and Benny have already told me about the sign stealing," he announced.

"What?" said Sam Jackson.

"Impossible!" said Winn.

"Not at all impossible," Grandfather replied. "My grandchildren have solved mysteries before."

Jessie explained why they thought someone was stealing the Cogs' signs and giving them to Cody Howard. Sam and Mr. Tanaka nodded their heads as Jessie talked.

But Winn shook his head. "There are ten thousand people out there," he said. "Even if there is a spy, how are you going to know who it is?"

Henry spoke. "We think there are only four suspects," he said.

"*Four?*" Winn held up four fingers and then pretended to faint.

Henry didn't like the way Winn was making fun of them. "We hope we can figure out which one is the spy during tomorrow's game," he told Mr. Tanaka.

"Who are these four suspects?" Sam Jackson demanded. "If what you say is true, let's keep all four of them out of the ballpark!"

"No, Sam, that's not right," replied Mr. Tanaka. "We would be keeping three innocent people away from the game."

"I don't care!" shouted the manager.

Mr. Tanaka looked at the Aldens. "Please," he said, "tell us who your four suspects are." "Three of them sit in the bleachers," said Benny, "and one sits right next to the Cogs dugout."

"*What?!*" said Mr. Tanaka, very upset. "No, that can't be."

Everybody waited for Mr. Tanaka to say something more, but he just stared at the top of his desk.

"The person who sits next to the Cogs dugout can't see the catcher's signs," Jessie said. "But he can hear what you're saying in the dugout," she told the manager. "And he's always writing in a small notebook."

"And he speaks into a headphone," added

Henry. "He might be talking to somebody who's somewhere else in the ballpark."

"Kick him out!" Sam Jackson shouted to Mr. Tanaka, who just shook his head.

"The three people in the bleachers can all see the catcher's signs," Henry explained. "And they all make motions that might be signals."

Sam Jackson lifted his baseball cap and rubbed his head again. "Tell me about these three. Who are they? What kind of motions do they make?"

Jessie told him about Emma Larke, one of the suspects. "Yesterday she wore a visor and stood up and waved it when Cody Howard came to bat. Today she wore a straw hat and did the same thing."

Violet told him about Carlos Garcia. "He's easy to see because his baseball cap has an antenna wire with a tall pennant at the top. Whenever Cody comes to bat, Carlos bangs the lid of his hot dog box."

"The third suspect is Wheelie the mascot," said Henry. "He sits in the best position to steal the signs. And every time Cody comes to bat, Wheelie holds his nose."

Sam Jackson looked at the children, then looked at Winn. "*Wheelie?*" he asked. "You can't be serious!"

Winn pretended to sob and wipe tears from his eyes.

"Cut it out, Winn." The manager was annoyed. "You kids are very observant. Based on what you've told me, it's obvious who the spy is—Emma Larke."

"Who is she?" asked Mr. Tanaka. "And why is it obvious?"

"Ah, she was dating Reese Dawkins," Sam Jackson answered. "But he broke up with her, and now she hates him and the Cogs. Emma wants to make Reese look bad," he argued. "What better way than to steal his signs and give them to Cody Howard? She doesn't want Reese to win the batting championship."

"We didn't know that Emma used to date Reese," said Jessie. "That gives her a motive."

"But it doesn't prove that she's the spy," said Violet softly.

"She might be the spy," said Winn, who was now serious. "But you have to consider Carlos, too."

"I like Carlos," said Mr. Tanaka. "He's a good worker and a cheerful person. Why in the world would he steal our signs?"

"I know why," said Winn.

"I know why, too." Sam Jackson said. "Carlos is a good ball player. He tried out for the team this past spring. Carlos wanted to be catcher. He was good… but just not good enough. We signed Reese Dawkins instead."

"I think it's Carlos," said Winn. "He wants to make Reese look bad so that the Cogs will accept him at the next tryout."

Benny spoke up. "Why does Carlos give you envelopes during the game?" he asked Winn.

"Envelopes?" asked Mr. Tanaka. "What envelopes?"

"The kid is crazy," said Winn. "Carlos doesn't give me any envelopes."

Jessie, Violet, and Henry all shook their heads. "Yes, he does," said Jessie. "We've all seen Carlos bring you hot dogs and soft drinks. And sometimes he pulls an envelope out of his pocket and hands it to you."

Mr. Tanaka looked at Winn. "What is this about?" he demanded. "You aren't taking money from the fans, are you? I pay you well, and you must never take money from the fans. Everything that Wheelie does must be free to the fans."

Winn nodded his head. "I can explain," he said. "I forgot about the envelopes. There's nothing in them but notes. They're notes from the fans."

"What kind of notes?" asked Mr. Tanaka.

"The fans write down ideas on what kind of stunts I should do," answered Wheelie. "Some of them want me to skip rope, for example. I can't do that, I'd trip and break my neck."

"Hmmm," said Mr. Tanaka, rubbing his chin. "It does not seem like a good idea."

Henry and Benny looked at each other. They knew that Wheelie asked for money when Henry had asked for an autograph.

"Should we say something?" Benny whispered to Henry.

Henry shook his head. Wheelie liked to joke a lot. Maybe Wheelie had been joking with him about the autograph. For all Henry knew, maybe Wheelie was telling the truth about the envelopes.

Mr. Tanaka looked at everybody in the room. "We all agree that somebody is stealing signs."

Everybody nodded.

"And we agree that we have no proof of who it is." Mr. Tanaka went on.

Everybody agreed.

"If the spy isn't discovered and stopped, the Cogs will not win the pennant this year."

CHAPTER 5

Back to the Bleachers

That night, Grandfather and the children ate dinner at the inn where they were staying. After dinner, the children talked in their room.

"Winn said the envelopes he gets don't have money in them," said Benny. "But Henry and I saw money fall out of an envelope in his pocket."

"Yes," added Henry. "There were lots of one-hundred dollar bills in the envelope. I don't think anybody would pay a hundred dollars for a Wheelie autograph."

"Me, neither!" shouted Benny.

"We didn't know that Reese Dawkins used to be Emma's boyfriend," said Jessie. "I think she wants him to fail at his job as catcher."

"We didn't know that Carlos wants to be the Cogs catcher," added Henry. "He also wants to see Reese fail."

"Mr. Tanaka was very upset when we mentioned Mr. X," said Violet. "I wonder why."

"Wheelie was making fun of us," said Benny. "It's not nice to make fun of people."

"You're right, Benny, it's not," said Jessie.

"Tomorrow is the third of the five games," Henry said. "Tomorrow we have to figure out which of our suspects is the spy."

* * * *

The next morning the children walked straight to the owner's office.

"We would like to help you again today," they told Mr. Tanaka.

"Thank you," he said, "but I think the best way you can help me is to find the spy. So

I would like you to spend all the time you need doing that. Where would you like to sit today?"

The Aldens had talked it over the night before. They told Mr. Tanaka that they needed to sit in the bleachers. He handed them tickets to the same four seats they'd had the first day.

"Before you go," said Mr. Tanaka, "there's something I must tell you."

The children waited.

Mr. Tanaka cleared his throat. "Yesterday I did not tell you something—something I should have told you. It is about the man you call Mr. X."

"What about him?" asked Violet, who could see that Mr. Tanaka was having trouble talking about this.

"Mr. X is really Simon Brock. Do you know who Simon Brock is?"

Henry, Jessie, Violet, and Benny all shook their heads.

"He's a famous movie producer," said Mr. Tanaka. "He grew up in Clayton. For three summers, he was batboy for the Clayton Cogs. Now he likes to come back each summer and watch the games. He's a big Cogs fan."

"We could tell that he likes the Cogs," said Henry. "But why did he want us to call him Mr. X?"

"Simon Brock doesn't want to be recognized," explained Mr. Tanaka. "He's afraid that if anybody knows who he is, they'll bother him. So many people want to be movie stars, they might not let Mr. Brock watch the game in peace."

Jessie nodded. "What is Mr. X—I mean, Mr. Brock—doing with a notebook and headphone?" she asked.

"Oh, that," laughed Mr. Tanaka. "He told me he's working on an idea for a new movie. Whenever he gets an idea, he writes it down. Or he records it by talking into his headphone."

"Wow!" said Benny. "He must be working on a baseball movie!"

Everybody looked at Benny. "Why do you say that?" asked Mr. Tanaka.

"Because every time something exciting

happens in the game, Mr. Tanaka takes out his notebook," said Benny. "Or he talks into his headphone."

"Hmmm," said Mr. Tanaka. "Well, if he is working on a movie, I hope he films it in Cogwheel Stadium."

* * * *

"We're down to three suspects," said Jessie. "Each of us should watch one person very closely."

"I'll watch Emma Larke," said Violet.

"I'll watch Wheelie," said Henry.

"And I'll watch Carlos Garcia," said Jessie.

"I'll watch the game," said Benny. "I want the Cogs to win!"

The others laughed. "*Somebody* has to watch the game," said Henry.

· "It's an important job," said Benny. "Do you think we have time for some hot dogs before we begin work?"

"There's Carlos," said Jessie as Carlos walked toward them.

"Hello," said Carlos. "Ready for some red hots?" he asked.

"We're hungry," said Henry. "We'd like eight hot dogs."

"Good choice!" said Carlos with a smile. "If I remember right, all four of you like mustard." He topped their dogs with mustard and passed two hot dogs to each of the children.

"Do you think the Cogs will win today?" Jessie asked him.

Carlos no longer smiled. In fact, he looked very sad. "I don't think so," he said. "Every time Cody Howard comes to bat, Reese Dawkins calls the wrong pitch."

"Is it true that you tried out for the team?" asked Jessie.

"Who told you that?!" Carlos looked at them suspiciously.

"We heard Sam Jackson, the manager, say so," said Jessie.

"Oh," said Carlos. "Yes, it's true. The manager didn't pick me. But look at the bad job Reese is doing—I'll bet Sam Jackson picks me next year."

Carlos walked up the aisle to sell more hot

dogs. The Aldens ate their food.

A woman in tan pants and a light trench-coat sat down in front of them. She wore dark sunglasses and a big hat with a brim.

Violet thought they were strange clothes to wear on a hot summer day.

The woman turned around and said, "Hello to all of you."

Violet realized that the young woman was Emma Larke.

The Aldens said hello. Violet asked Emma if she thought the Cogs would win today.

"No," said Emma sadly. "I don't think so."

Violet didn't understand why Emma looked sad. Didn't Emma want the Cogs to lose?

Carlos returned and said hello to Emma. He sold her a hot dog. As he handed it to her, she whispered something to him. Carlos smiled.

Henry saw Wheelie coming down the aisle. Every few steps Wheelie did a little dance.

When he reached the Aldens, Wheelie sank to his knees. He clasped his hands together as if begging. He shook his head back and forth. Then Wheelie stood up and pointed a hand down toward Emma Larke's head. Wheelie nodded his head up and down. Wheelie was telling them that he thought Emma was the sign stealer.

Wheelie went to his special platform and sat down. Carlos brought him a hot dog and a soft drink.

"Yesterday Winn thought Carlos was the sign stealer," Henry told the others. "I wonder what made him change his mind?

The game began. When Reese Dawkins came to bat, Emma stood up and pointed at him. "You're history," she growled in a deep voice. "You're gone, Reese Dawkins. Gone!"

"Look," Benny whispered to Violet. "She's pointing with her left hand."

"Yes," said Violet. "I noticed that Emma is left-handed.

"Maybe she's the one who wrote Wheelie's name on that envelope," said Henry. He remembered the funny slanted handwriting.

Reese Dawkins hit a home run right at Emma. She ducked, and so did everybody else around her. Wheelie turned three cartwheels on his platform. The Cogs were leading, 1-0.

When Cody Howard came to bat, Emma stood again. She pulled her hat lower on her head and thrust out her arm. She pointed at Cody and growled, "Get the job done, Cody!"

Jessie watched Carlos, who stood staring at Cody Howard. Carlos banged the lid of his hot dog box three times.

Henry watched Wheelie, who was leaning back in his special chair. Wheelie looked like he was relaxing and wasn't worried.

Cody Howard smashed a triple and drove in one run.

"What if there are two sign stealers?" asked Jessie. "What if Carlos and Emma are a team?"

"Or Carlos and Wheelie," said Henry.

"What if we can't prove who it is?" said Violet.

The children looked at each other. They had promised Mr. Tanaka and Sam Jackson that they would discover who was stealing signs. What if they just couldn't find the proof?

The Cogs lost the game, 2-1.

The Aldens watched as the fans started to leave.

Violet noticed that Emma Larke did not look happy. But if Emma wanted the Hatters to win, shouldn't she be happy?

Jessie noticed that Carlos slumped down into an empty seat. He looked very sad.

Henry watched Wheelie walk away. It was impossible to see inside Wheelie's costume, to see if he was happy or sad.

CHAPTER 6

Mr. X Explains

At the top of the aisle, Henry and Jessie went in one direction. Violet and Benny went in the other. They hoped to find Mr. X before he left the ballpark.

But ten minutes later, neither group had found Mr. X.

"What should we do now?" asked Violet when they all met up again.

"Let's go outside," answered Jessie.

So they left the stadium, which was still crowded with fans. Unhappy fans, because

the Cogs had lost three games in a row to the Hatters. The Cogs *had* to win the last two games. If they didn't, they would lose the pennant race to the their biggest rival.

"There he is," said Benny. He pointed to a souvenir stand.

Mr. X stood there, holding three different kinds of Cogs baseball caps.

"Hello," said Jessie.

Mr. X turned. "Why, hello," he said.

"We need to talk to you about the sign stealing," said Henry.

"Sure," said Mr. X. He chose one of the hats and paid for it. "Let's step out of the crowd," he said. He led them to the shade of a tree.

"What made you decide that signs are being stolen?" Jessie asked him.

"That's easy," replied Mr. X. "It's clear to anybody who knows baseball well. Cody Howard knows which pitch is coming next. He waits for just the right pitch. Then he hits a triple or home run and the Hatters win the game." Mr. X looked at them closely. "Why are the four of you so interested?" he asked.

"We're working for Mr. Tanaka," Jessie explained.

"We told Mr. Tanaka we had three solid suspects," Jessie explained. "Plus one not-so-likely suspect."

"That was you," Henry added.

"*Me?!*" Mr. X said. "Why me?"

"Because you're always taking notes at the game," said Violet. "And then you speak into your headphone."

Mr. X smiled. He pulled out his notebook and wrote in it. Then he spoke into his headphone.

"New idea," he said. "Four kid detectives try to discover who's stealing signs."

Mr. X looked at the Aldens. "You all look trustworthy," he said, "so keep what I'm telling you a secret. My name is Simon Brock. I'm a movie producer."

Henry nodded. "We know," he said. "When we mentioned you as a suspect, Mr. Tanaka told us who you are."

"So," said Simon Brock, "I'm off the

suspect list because I'm a movie producer?"

Jessie shook her head. "No," she said. "You're off the suspect list because you can't see the catcher's signs. And Cody Howard can't see you when he's at bat."

Simon Brock laughed and spoke into his headphone. "The kid detectives are very smart," he said. "They solve the case." He smiled. "You're giving me great ideas for a new movie," he told them.

Henry nodded. "We just want to know why you think Emma Larke is stealing signs."

"Who?" asked Simon Brock.

"Emma Larke," said Violet. "Yesterday she was wearing a lavender dress. You pointed to her and said she was stealing signs."

"Right!" said Mr. Brock. "I didn't know her name. Yes," he said, "she's the one who's stealing signs."

"Why are you so sure?" Henry asked again.

"She's so easy to see," explained Mr. Brock. "She calls attention to herself. She wears very different clothing each day."

"Did you see Emma do anything today

that made you think she was stealing signs?" asked Violet.

Mr. Brock rubbed his jaw. "She did the same things she always does," he said. "She stands up when Cody Howard comes to bat. She shouts something. She waves her hat. Then Cody hits a home run or a triple. That might mean something, but I don't know what."

"Neither do we," confessed Henry. "We wanted to figure out who the spy was today. But we still have the same three suspects."

"Who are the other two?" asked Simon Brock.

"We don't want to say," Violet explained.

Mr. Brock nodded. "Spoken like true detectives," he said. Then he sat down on a bench. "This is serious stuff," he said. "The Cogs must win both of the last two games. If there's anything I can do to help you, just let me know."

* * * *

"Why so glum?" Grandfather asked at dinner.

"We haven't discovered who the spy is," explained Violet. "At today's game we watched all three very closely. But we couldn't tell which one was stealing signs."

"All three do things when Cody Howard is at bat," Henry explained. "Things that could be signals."

"We promised Mr. Tanaka we would help," said Jessie. "But we're getting nowhere."

"I'm sure that's not true," said Grandfather. "You are all very good thinkers. You must be getting somewhere."

"If we could just rule out one of them," said Henry. "Then we would be down to two suspects."

"But we still wouldn't know which of the two *is* the spy," argued Jessie.

"We can't guess," said Violet. "That wouldn't be fair."

"But if we had only two suspects, we could isolate one," said Henry.

"*I-so-late?*" asked Benny. "What does that mean?"

"Remember when you had the measles?"

Jessie asked Benny. "You had to stay home. Nobody could come visit you. You were *isolated* so that other people wouldn't catch the measles from you."

Benny looked confused. "Are we going to put a suspect where nobody can see him?" he asked.

Henry laughed. "Something like that," he said. "If we can down to two suspects, we can put one of them where Cody Howard can't see him."

"Yes!" said Jessie excitedly. "Let's make a list of all the clues after dinner. I'm sure if we think hard, we can figure out who is innocent."

"That would leave us with two suspects," said Violet.

"Let's make our list right away," said Benny, looking around. "Right after dessert, I mean."

CHAPTER 7

Who Is the Spy?

The children had the inn's game room all to themselves. They sat at one of the tables and Jessie pulled out her notebook.

"Do we all agree that Simon Brock isn't a suspect any more?" she asked.

Henry, Violet, and Benny nodded their heads. "He's just enjoying the baseball games," said Henry. "And thinking about movies."

"So," said Jessie, "let's begin with Carlos Garcia." She wrote his name in her notebook.

Then they discussed all the things that made it seem as if Carlos might be stealing signs. Jessie listed them.

Carlos Garcia

• Carlos dislikes Reese Dawkins, the Cogs catcher, and wants to replace him.

• Carlos hands Winn envelopes during the ballgame — maybe he and Winn are working together to steal signs.

• Carlos put an envelope into Emma's straw bag.

• Carlos and Emma talk about Reese Dawkins. They both want to see Reese Dawkins fail. Maybe Carlos and Emma are working together to steal signs.

• Carlos wears a pennant on his cap: he can be seen all the way across the ballpark.

• Every time Cody Howard comes to bat, Carlos bangs the lid of his vendor's box up and down. Could this be a signal to Cody?

"This looks bad," said Henry. "Carlos does a lot of suspicious things."

"We can't prove that Carlos is stealing signs," said Jessie. "And we can't prove that he's not stealing them."

"What about Emma Larke?" asked Benny.

Jessie made a new list.

Emma Larke

• She dislikes Reese Dawkins, the Cogs catcher, and wants to see him fail.

• She wears things that make it easy for the batter to see her.

• Whenever Cody Howard comes to bat, Emma stands up and shouts and waves her hat. This could be a signal to Cody.

• She was talking to Carlos Garcia about Reese Dawkins, the catcher.

• She received an envelope from Carlos Garcia.

"Emma is doing a lot of suspicious-looking things," said Violet.

"Maybe the things she's doing are *too* suspicious," said Henry.

"What do you mean?" asked Benny.

"Well," said Henry to his younger brother, "if you were stealing signs, wouldn't you try to hide it?"

Benny thought about this. "I would never steal," he said. "But a person who steals tries to hide it."

"Emma doesn't seem to hide what she's doing," said Violet.

"Let's go to our last suspect," said Henry.

"Winn Winchell," said Jessie as she wrote the name. "The team mascot."

"Also known as Wheelie," Benny said.

The others laughed.

The children spent a long time discussing Wheelie. Jessie wrote the list.

Wheelie

• Wheelie receives envelopes from Carlos during the game. Maybe Wheelie and Carlos are working together to steal signs.

• Wheelie has a very clear view of the catcher's signals.

• Wheelie makes motions each time Cody Howard is at bat. Sometimes he holds his nose, sometimes he holds both hands out to the side.

• Wheelie seems to want money. He seems

to want fans to pay for autographs.

• Benny and Henry saw an envelope with money in it fall out of Wheelie's pocket.

"This is a tough mystery to solve," Violet said. "All three people look guilty."

Henry stood up and paced around. "I wish we had been able to figure out who the spy was today."

"Me, too," said Benny. "But all three of them did the same things they always do."

"I am very sad," said Violet. "We don't have a name to give Mr. Tanaka tomorrow morning. That means the spy will continue spying. And that means the Cogs will lose tomorrow's game."

"But," said Henry, still walking back and forth, "I think we can tell who's *not* guilty."

Jessie nodded. "Yes. Who do you think is innocent, Benny?"

"Emma." said Benny. "Because she doesn't hide what she's doing."

"Very good," said Jessie with a smile.

"I think Emma is innocent, too" said Violet. "And I think I know why she wears different clothes. We can ask her tomorrow."

"Then we will have two suspects," said Jessie. "Carlos and Wheelie."

"We will *i-so-late* one of them," said Benny. "Like when I had the measles."

Henry sat back down. "This will be the most important decision we make," he said. "If we isolate the right person, nobody will be there to give stolen signs to Cody Howard."

"That means the Cogs will have a fair chance to win the game," said Jessie.

"We can think about this while we sleep," said Violet. "In the morning we can decide who to isolate."

The others agreed.

"There's one more thing we can do," said Jessie.

"What's that?" asked Henry.

"We can get two autographs. I'll get one, and Benny can get the other one."

"Good thinking," said Henry. "The autographs will help us."

CHAPTER 8

Emma's Clothes

The next morning the children went to Cogwheel Stadium with Grandfather. They arrived so early they had time to play in the ballpark outside the stadium. As soon as they saw cars arriving for the game, the Aldens put away their bats and balls.

Just inside Cogwheel Stadium, they waited for Emma Larke to show up. "I wonder what Emma will be wearing today?" said Benny.

They saw her coming through the turnstile. Today she was wearing a Cogs baseball cap, an orange Cogs baseball shirt, and white baseball pants.

"I thought Emma hated the Cogs," whispered Jessie.

"Emma looks very sad," said Violet.

Henry said hello and asked Emma if they could talk to her.

"Talk?" said Emma. "What about?"

Before Henry could start asking the questions they needed to ask, Benny blurted out, "Why are you wearing a Cogs uniform?"

Emma started to cry. "I'm a Cogs fan, really I am. I should have been rooting for them all along. And now," she said, crying harder, "the Cogs won't win the pennant. It's all my fault!"

"How is it your fault?" asked Jessie.

"I rooted for Cody Howard," said Emma, "just because I was so mad at Reese Dawkins! And look what happened—every time I cheered for Cody, he hit a home run! Or a triple! If only I hadn't cheered for him."

Emma wiped tears from her eyes. "It's all my fault," she repeated.

"It's not your fault," said Henry, "unless you were telling Cody which pitch was coming."

Emma stopped crying and looked at Henry. "Huh?" she said. "You mean like in sign stealing?"

"Yes," said Jessie, "that's what we mean."

Emma looked at the Aldens without saying anything. She seemed to be thinking. "Do you mean somebody is stealing signs and giving them to Cody?" she asked.

"Yes," said Henry, "that's what somebody is doing."

Suddenly Emma's eyes grew wide. "So you think I've been stealing signs?"

"Are you?" asked Jessie.

"No!" shouted Emma, who was now angry. "Why do you think it's me?"

"You wear a lot of different hats," said Benny. "And you wave them around when Cody comes to bat. Then he gets a big hit."

Emma became silent. The children waited

for her to speak, but she didn't say anything. Finally Henry asked, "Why do you stand up and wave your hat whenever Cody is at bat?"

"I want to explain," said Emma, "but I can't."

"Why not?" asked Henry.

"Because it involves another person," said Emma. "Somebody I shouldn't be talking about."

"That's okay," said Violet. "I know what you mean."

Emma stared at Violet. "You do?"

Violet smiled shyly. "Yes," she said. "The other person is Simon Brock."

All sadness vanished from Emma Larke's face. Her eyes lit up. She smiled happily. "Do the four of you *know* Simon Brock? I saw you *sitting right next to him* two games ago!"

"Yes, we know Mr. Brock," Jessie replied. "We know that he's a movie producer."

"Shhhh!" warned Emma, putting her finger to her lips. "Mr. Brock doesn't want anybody to know who he is. He wants to watch the games without being bothered."

"That's true," said Henry, "but how do you know that?"

"Oh," said Emma, twirling a lock of her hair around a finger, "I read film magazines all the time. I've seen photos of Simon Brock, so I recognized him in line one day. And," she said, "I could tell by how he dresses that he doesn't want people to know who he is. You know, the baseball cap pulled low, and the dark sunglasses."

"I know why you wear different clothes every day," Violet told Emma. "I know why you stand up and wave your hat."

Emma looked at Violet and smiled. "I believe you *do* know," she said.

"You want Mr. Brock to notice you," Violet said. "You want to be a movie star."

"Yes!" shouted Emma, clapping her hands together. "I want Simon Brock to see that I can act many different roles. One day I was an average fan. The next day I was a Southern lady. Yesterday I was a gangster! And today I'm a diehard Cogs fan."

Emma changed from happy to worried.

"Do you think that Mr. Brock has noticed me?" she asked.

"Yes," Henry answered. "He has definitely noticed you." Henry did not tell Emma that Simon Brock suspected her of being the sign stealer.

"Oh!" shouted Emma. "That's wonderful!" She became quiet and looked at Henry, Jessie, Violet, and Benny. "Do you think... do you think that you could introduce me to Mr. Brock?" she begged.

"Sure," said Jessie, "if you answer one question for us."

"Okay," Emma said. "What question?"

"We saw Carlos Garcia slip an envelope into your purse two days ago," Jessie explained. "What was in the envelope?"

Emma Larke blushed. "Oh, that," she said. "That was a note from Carlos asking me for a date."

"Thank you," said Henry. "We'll introduce you to Mr. Brock, but first we have a meeting with Mr. Tanaka."

* * * *

"Emma Larke looked guilty," said Jessie as the four of them walked to the owner's office. "But she *isn't* guilty. So now we're down to two suspects."

"But if Carlos wrote a letter asking Emma for a date, maybe he's innocent, too," said Violet.

"Maybe," Henry replied. "But remember that Carlos also gives envelopes to Wheelie. We don't know what's in those envelopes."

When the children entered Mr. Tanaka's office, they found him walking back and forth, back and forth.

"At last!" he said when he saw them. "Who's the spy?"

"It's not Simon Brock," Jessie told him. "And it's not Emma Larke."

"So," said Mr. Tanaka. "Is it Carlos Garcia? Or is it Wheelie?"

"We can't prove which of them is the spy," said Henry.

Mr. Tanaka sat in his chair and put his head in his hands. "Then it's all over," he moaned. "The Hatters will win."

Henry shook his head. "No. We have a plan to prove whether the spy is Carlos or Wheelie."

Mr. Tanaka looked up. "You do?" he asked, studying the children.

"Yes," said Jessie. "In order to prove which one is the spy, we have to separate them. We have to stop either Carlos or Wheelie from being where they can see the signs."

"And where Cody can see the spy," added Violet.

Mr. Tanaka thought about this a while. "It's a good plan," he said. "Which one should we take out of the bleachers?" he asked.

"We've talked about this," said Henry, "and we think Wheelie should leave the bleachers."

"Hmmm," said Mr. Tanaka, rubbing his chin. "I will invite Winn Winchell to sit with me in the owner's box today. In fact, I will *insist* that he sit with me."

"That's good," said Henry. "Do you have another person to play Wheelie?"

Mr. Tanaka looked at him. "Yes," he said,

"I certainly do."

"Good," said Jessie. "But if Cody Howard hits a home run the first time he comes to bat, you must act fast."

Mr. Tanaka nodded. "Excellent plan," he said. "If Cody hits a home run, then the spy is Carlos. I will have Carlos removed from the bleachers immediately, so that he won't be able to signal to Cody for the rest of the game."

Mr. Tanaka picked up his telephone and spoke to his assistant. "Have Winn Winchell come to my office," he said. "Immediately!"

In less than five minutes, Winn Winchell walked into the owner's office. As he walked in, the Aldens walked out.

CHAPTER 9

The World Looks Orange

Violet and Benny hurried to their seats in the bleachers. They sat behind Emma once again.

"Hi," said Emma, turning around. "Where are Henry and Jessie?"

"Jessie is getting an autograph," said Benny. "I'm going to get one, too."

"It's fun to get autographs," said Emma. "Whose autograph do you want?"

Benny looked all around. "I want Carlos's autograph," he said.

Emma laughed. "Carlos will be *thrilled* that you want his autograph, Benny!" She looked around. "Is Henry getting an autograph, too?"

"No," said Violet. "Henry is sitting in a different seat today."

"Oh," said Emma. "Well, I hope it's a good seat. I wouldn't want him to miss this game. The Cogs *must* win." She pounded the arms of her chair.

Violet and Benny looked all around, taking in the sights and smelling the hot dogs. Soon Jessie arrived.

"Got it!" she said, showing them a scorecard. Jessie tucked the scorecard into her pocket. "I'm hungry," she said, looking around. "And here comes Carlos."

Jessie bought hot dogs for Violet, Benny, and herself. She paid Carlos and gave him a tip.

"Thanks," said Carlos. "Where's Henry?"

"Oh, he's around here somewhere," said Jessie. She didn't want to say where he was.

Suddenly Benny jumped up. "It's Wheelie!"

he shouted, pointing down to the field. The big, fuzzy, orange mascot ran across the field, tossing rolled-up T-shirts to the fans.

"Wheelie!" shouted Benny. "Up here!"

Emma smiled at Benny. "I didn't know you liked Wheelie so much," she said.

"I love Wheelie," replied Benny.

Just then the mascot threw a rolled-up T-shirt toward their seats. The large cotton bundle came right at Emma. But Emma ducked at the last minute, and Benny caught the T-shirt.

All the fans applauded Benny. "Nice catch!" they shouted.

Benny was very excited. He unwrapped the T-shirt and held it up. Wheelie's picture was on the front.

"I'm going to ask Wheelie to autograph my shirt," said Benny.

Jessie and Violet smiled.

Emma frowned. "I don't know," she said. "Wheelie doesn't seem to like to autograph things."

Down on the field, Wheelie was jumping

up and down. He pumped both arms into the air. He spread his fingers in a *V* for victory. And then Wheelie did cartwheels all the way back to his special door.

The Cogs fans went wild. They applauded long and loud. "Go, Cogs, go!" they shouted. "Cogs will win! Cogs will win!" Of all the fans, Emma Larke shouted the loudest.

Benny kept looking back, to the top of the aisle. He waited for Wheelie. And then he saw the mascot at the top of the stairs.

Wheelie stopped to slap hands with fans. Whenever a fan handed him something to sign, Wheelie autographed it.

"Well, look at that," said Emma. "Wheelie is autographing everything!"

It took Wheelie a long time to reach the bottom of the aisle. Finally he reached the row where Jessie, Violet, and Benny were. He autographed Benny's T-shirt.

"Thank you," said Benny.

Carlos patted Wheelie on an orange shoulder. "Way to go, Wheelie. That's the right thing to do."

Wheelie climbed over the railing to his special platform and special seat.

The game began!

* * * *

From inside the mascot's costume, Henry thought the world looked orange. That was because one of Wheelie's orange eyelashes was drooping in front of the eye opening. Everything Henry saw from that eye looked a bit orange-y.

Mr. Tanaka had asked Henry to take Winn Winchell's place inside the mascot costume.

"But I've never been a mascot before," Henry had said. "I'm not sure I'd know what to do."

"You will do a great job," Mr. Tanaka had said. "And you will be helping the team."

So Henry had gone to Wheelie's dressing room and taken off his shirt and shoes. Just as he finished putting on the mascot's costume, there was a knock on the door.

Henry had opened the door. A boy about his age was there. He wore a Hatter's uniform. He handed Wheelie an envelope.

Henry took the envelope, but he didn't say anything. He knew Wheelie did not talk.

The boy turned and walked away quickly. Henry saw the words *Hatters Batboy* written across the back of the boy's uniform.

The envelope that Henry was holding was full of something papery. The handwriting on it said *Wheelie*. The handwriting slanted to the left! Henry put the envelope in one of the pockets of his shorts. Then he went out onto the field to throw T-shirts to the fans.

It's fun playing Wheelie, thought Henry, as he settled into his special chair.

The Cogs pitcher struck out the first Hatter, walked the second, and got the third to hit into a double play. In the bottom of the first inning, Reese Dawkins hit a home run with a runner on base. Henry stood up and did five cartwheels across the platform. Then he jumped up and down and pumped his arms in the air. The Cogs were leading, 2-0!

In the top of the second inning, Cody Howard was the first Hatter to bat.

Henry sat in the special chair. He put both feet flat on the platform. He crossed his arms and sat very, very still. Henry knew that if Cody Howard hit a home run, it meant that Carlos was stealing the signs.

Henry stared at Cody. It seemed like Cody Howard was staring right back at him! Of course Cody didn't know he was looking at Henry, since Henry was dressed as Wheelie. Cody hit a foul ball on the first pitch. He looked out toward the bleachers. He pointed his bat at the bleachers, then pounded it on home plate.

Henry heard a *clang-clang-clang* behind him. Carlos was banging the lid of his hot dog box up and down.

Now Henry realized what Carlos was doing. Carlos wanted to upset Cody Howard and make him miss! *Carlos is a true Cogs fan,* thought Henry.

Cody swung at the second pitch and missed.

The Cogs fans cheered loudly.

Cody stepped out of the batter's box and

walked around. Finally the umpire made him step back into the box. Cody pointed his bat toward the bleachers.

Henry did not move a muscle. He sat as still as a statue. He knew Cody wanted Wheelie to tell him what pitch was coming.

Cody swung and missed.

"You're out!" shouted the umpire. Cody walked back to the Hatters dugout. He glared toward the bleachers.

Carlos tapped Wheelie on the shoulder and handed him a hot dog and soft drink. "I love your new style, Wheelie! The fans love the jumps!" Carlos bent low so only Wheelie could hear him, "I'm glad to see you're signing autographs for free. That's what a mascot should do."

Henry nodded. He looked at his hot dog. *How am I going to eat this with a costume on?* he wondered.

The Cogs didn't score in the second or third innings. Neither did the Hatters. The score stood at 2-0. In the top of the fifth, Cody Howard came to bat again.

Once again Henry sat very still. His feet were flat on the platform. His arms were folded against his chest.

Once again Cody Howard seemed to be looking straight at him. Cody pointed his bat and pounded the plate. Henry could see Reese Dawkins hold down two fingers: curve ball. Henry watched the pitcher release the ball. He watched it zoom toward the plate, then curve. He saw Cody Howard swing and miss.

Cody pounded his bat on the plate. He pointed his bat at the bleachers. He scowled.

Wow, thought Henry. Cody is so angry that even if I signaled what pitch was coming, he would swing and miss.

Swing and miss is what Cody did. Strike two.

Cody tried to blast the next pitch out of the park — but his bat hit only air.

"You're out!" shouted the umpire.

Wheelie jumped up and down. He pumped his arms. The fans roared their approval.

"I love the Cogs!" shouted Emma Larke.

"Go, Cogs!" shouted Carlos. "Go for the pennant!"

"Yay, Cogs!" shouted Benny. "Yay, Wheelie!"

Cody Howard did not get a hit at all. The Cogs won the game, 4-0.

When Henry climbed back over the rail and stood in the aisles, he was mobbed by fans. Some wanted his autograph, which he gave. Others just wanted to pat him on the back.

Wheelie waited until all the fans had left. Then he and Jessie and Violet and Benny walked to the owner's box.

* * * *

Mr. Tanaka, Grandfather, and Winn Winchell all sat in the owner's box.

Jessie saw how happy Mr. Tanaka looked. Grandfather looked happy, too. Winn Winchell did not look happy.

"Henry!" said Mr. Tanaka, jumping up. "You were wonderful!" He helped Henry take off the top half of the Wheelie costume.

"I caught a Wheelie T-shirt!" said Benny,

pulling the shirt over his head. "And I got Wheelie's autograph, too," he said, pointing to where Henry had signed the shirt *Wheelie*.

"Yeah, yeah," growled Winn Winchell. "So the kids all had fun." He pointed at Henry and said, "But this kid can't play Wheelie like I can."

Winn jumped up and clenched his fists. "Tomorrow *I'm* the mascot again," he said.

"No," said Mr. Tanaka, "you're not."

"What?!" Winn shouted. "I'm the mascot! This kid isn't the mascot!"

"The Cogs won today," Mr. Tanaka said to Winn. "The Cogs and Hatters are tied for first place. Whoever wins tomorrow wins the pennant."

"What's that got to do with the mascot?" demanded Winn.

Mr. Tanaka pointed at a chair. "Sit down," he told Winn.

Winn glared at the owner, but finally Winn sat down.

"The Cogs have lost games they should have won," said Mr. Tanaka, his voice stern.

"The Cogs have lost because somebody was stealing signs."

"Stealing signs isn't a fair way to win," said Benny.

Winn waved his hand at them. "It's got nothing to do with me."

"Yes, it does," said Henry. "You're the sign stealer."

"You're crazy," answered Winn.

Henry reached into a pocket and pulled out an envelope. "Today the Hatters batboy came to Wheelie's dressing room. When I was in costume, he handed me this envelope."

"That's mine!" shouted Winn, jumping up.

But before Winn could grab the envelope, Mr. Tanaka stepped forward and took it from Henry's hand.

CHAPTER 10

The Spy Is Out

"Give me that!" shouted Winn. "It's mine!"

Mr. Tanaka ignored the shouts. He opened the envelope and pulled out what was inside.

"Money," said Mr. Tanaka. "One-hundred dollar bills." He counted the bills. "Ten of them!" Mr. Tanaka glared at Winn. "What is this money for?" he demanded.

"The money is from Carlos Garcia," said Winn. "Carlos wanted me to steal the signs and give them to Cody Howard. I refused."

"That's not true," said Benny.

"You don't know what you're talking about," growled Winn.

Henry spoke up. "The writing on the envelope isn't Carlos's handwriting."

"Yes, it is!" Winn insisted. "Carlos is the sign stealer."

"Mr. Tanaka," said Benny, "we can prove that isn't Carlos's handwriting." Benny reached into his pocket and pulled out a clean napkin. "Today I asked Carlos for his autograph. I watched him sign this napkin. This is his handwriting."

Mr. Tanaka held the envelope in one hand and the napkin in the other. "Carlos Garcia's handwriting does not match the handwriting on the envelope," he said.

Jessie spoke. "I also got an autograph today," she said, handing Mr. Tanaka a scorecard. "I asked Cody Howard to sign my scorecard," she said. "And he did."

Mr. Tanaka held the scorecard in one hand and the envelope in the other. "The handwriting is the same," he said.

"Okay, okay," said Winn Winchell. "So I was taking money from Cody. He wanted to win the batting title, and he was willing to pay me to help him."

"What you have done is dishonorable," said Mr. Tanaka. "You are fired," he added.

Mr. Tanaka opened the door. Four ballpark security guards stood in the hallway.

"Take Winn Winchell out of Cogwheel Stadium," said Mr. Tanaka. "Never let him come here again."

The guards escorted Winn Winchell out of the owner's box.

Mr. Tanaka waited until they were out of sight. Then he turned toward Henry, Jessie, Violet, and Benny. "Thank you so much for discovering who the spy was," he said. "And thank you also for all the other help you have given the Cogs and me."

"You're welcome," said Jessie. "We like to help."

"And we play fair," said Benny.

Mr. Tanaka smiled. "Tomorrow is the last game of the season," he said. "If the Hatters win, they will win the pennant. If the Cogs win, they will win the pennant. The game will be a fair game, with no sign stealing, thanks to the four of you."

"Do we get to watch the game?" asked Grandfather. "Or will we be in your office working on seating plans?" he teased his old friend.

"We will be sitting right here, in the owner's box," said Jim Tanaka. "And Jessie, Violet, and Benny will be with us."

Everybody looked at Henry.

"I know where I'll be," said Henry.

* * * *

The last game of the season was a night game. Grandfather couldn't park the car in his usual space because the stadium parking lot was so full.

"Are you adding more parking spaces for next year?" Violet asked him.

"Yes," said Grandfather. "And if the Cogs win the pennant tonight, I'll bet I have to add even *more* seats and parking spaces."

"I hope they win!" said Benny. He was

wearing his autographed Wheelie T-shirt.

Henry went to Wheelie's dressing room. Jessie, Violet, and Benny hurried to the owner's box with their grandfather.

The owner's box was above the ground seats of Cogwheel Stadium. It was just to one side of home plate.

"This is a great view," said Jessie, looking out at the ballpark through the open windows.

"Did we miss Henry?" asked Benny.

"Henry did a wonderful job as Wheelie," said Mr. Tanaka. "He gave away more T-shirts and water bottles than ever. Now he's on his way to the bleachers."

"Did he jump up and down and pump his arms?" asked Violet.

"Oh, yes," said Grandfather with a chuckle. "And the fans loved it."

"I think the players loved it, too," said Mr. Tanaka. "They think Wheelie brought them luck yesterday, so they're glad he's doing the same thing today."

A vendor came into the owner's box and set a large tray of hot dogs on a table.

"Please help yourselves," said Mr. Tanaka. Then the game began.

"You can see the whole ballpark from here," said Jessie.

"Yes, the owner's box has an excellent view," said Mr. Tanaka.

"You can see the whole stadium from the bleachers, too," said Benny.

Mr. Tanaka and Grandfather laughed. "Yes," admitted Mr. Tanaka, "you can."

Benny looked toward the bleachers and spotted Carlos Garcia. Benny waved, even though Carlos couldn't see him. Benny saw Wheelie sitting in his special chair on the platform. Benny waved. Wheelie waved back.

"There are so many interesting people in the bleachers," said Violet. She was looking at Emma Larke, who was wearing the same Cogs uniform she wore yesterday.

"Look!" said Violet. "That's Simon Brock sitting next to Emma Larke."

"It was very good of you children to introduce her to Mr. Brock," said Mr. Tanaka.

Violet watched Emma and Simon Brock.

They were talking to one another, and Mr. Brock was writing something in his notebook.

In the bottom of the second inning, Reese Dawkins hit a home run. The fans rose to their feet and clapped loudly. Wheelie turned five cartwheels in one direction, then five more in the opposite direction.

"Good," said Mr. Tanaka. "If Reese gets one more hit and Cody doesn't get any, Reese will win the batting title. And the car!"

Before he stepped into the dugout, Reese Dawkins waved toward the bleachers. Carlos Garcia waved back. So did Emma Larke. And so did Wheelie. The Cogs were leading, 1-0.

Even though Cody Howard didn't get a hit, the Hatters tied the score in the top of the ninth, 1-1.

In the bottom half of the ninth, the Cogs loaded the bases. There were two outs, and Reese Dawkins came to the plate.

Wheelie jumped up and down on his platform and pumped his arms. The fans jumped up and down and pumped their arms.

Reese Dawkins blasted the ball out of the stadium — a grand slam home run! The Cogs won the ball game, 5-1.

The Cogs won the pennant!

This time Wheelie did not turn cartwheels. This time, Wheelie did three backflips!

The players rushed out onto the field to celebrate. They lifted their caps toward the bleachers.

"Hmmm," said Mr. Tanaka. "I would be honored if you children would visit Cogwheel Stadium next year, too."

"I would love to see the Cogs play next year," said Jessie.

"I would love to catch another baseball," said Violet.

"And I would love to help Wheelie throw T-shirts and water bottles!" said Benny.